MW01222227

To Peggy
with every Good wish
from Lorna Page
(Vincent).

EBB AND FLOW

Eleven Short Stories

LORNA PAGE

authorHOUSE®

AuthorHouse™ UK Ltd.
500 Avebury Boulevard
Central Milton Keynes, MK9 2BE
www.authorhouse.co.uk
Phone: 08001974150

© 2009 Lorna Page. All rights reserved.

No part of this book may be reproduced, stored in a retrieval system, or
transmitted by any means without the written permission of the author.

First published by AuthorHouse   5/14/2009

ISBN: 978-1-4389-7767-6 (sc)

This book is printed on acid-free paper.

EBB and FLOW

I look long at the moving sea.
And the thought then slowly comes to me
That ebb and flow and ebb and flow –
Is surely the way that most lives go.

Around the rocks water eddies and bites
Swills and splashes, with dizzy delight
Throwing brilliant showers to sunny heights
Then passing to calmer waters, slow, steadying flow.

When beneath dark and lowering cloud
Raging – the flooding tide sweeps loud
Wild, engulfing, it lashes and tears
Oftimes, more than the land can bear.

The storm subsides. All spent and still,
Now gentle sea waves are a delicate rill.
With ebb and flow and ebb and flow
It's surely the way that most lives go.

*Written for me by my good friend Pat Magee,
and used by permission of her husband, Mac Magee*

*Lorna Page
Devon 2009*

Contents

Strangers

When Mrs. Mappin first saw the man he was sitting on a wooden bench looking out at the sea. The sun was shining but there was a wind blowing from the north east and the few seats placed in the lee of the wall were occupied by late holiday makers, grateful for the shelter which the wall provided.

There was just this one seat with a space on it for Mrs. Mappin. "Do you mind?" she said tentatively to the man; but he seemed not to hear, his eyes still fixed on the shifting waves.

She sat beside him and followed his gaze, just in case there was something happening which the man found so absorbing. There wasn't, and after a moment Mrs. Mappin fished in her handbag for the sun-shielding spectacles which she felt added an aura of mystery to her.

She was a friendly, talkative soul, and after a few minutes ventured, "Such a cold wind isn't it?"

It wasn't a profound statement and, rather to her surprise, the man turned his head towards her. "Yes," he remarked without interest.

Encouraged by this Mrs. Mappin enquired, "Are you staying here?" She thought he looked lonely and rather sad.

"Yes," he said again. "That is..." His voice trailed off into the wind and he fixed his eyes again on to the sea.

Mrs. Mappin was not a lady to give in after a first rebuff. "I live here," she said helpfully, and added, "My cottage is only a few minutes' walk away. My garden is filled with flowers. I love flowers," she said. "Do you?"

With apparent effort the man again withdrew his gaze from the waters and said, "Very much."

Fast blowing dark clouds suddenly hid the sun, turning the sea to a menacing grey.

"Oh, dear," said Mrs. Mappin. "It is cold. I could do with a nice hot cup of tea." She stood up and seemed about to wish the man a friendly goodbye. Instead she asked shyly, "I don't suppose you would like one too?"

He arose. "Might as well," he said.

He was taller than she expected, around five foot nine or ten she judged. Just a nice height, and he was good looking too - not that that mattered. She smiled a little to herself, thinking how her friend Amy would chide her for bringing home another complete stranger. "It's so dangerous, dear," she would say. "You never know..." She said that every time and it was always all right.

The man didn't talk much as he walked beside her, confining his conversation to monosyllables, while Mrs. Mappin chatted on about her cottage and garden.

It was a pretty garden, her pride and joy. Shielded from the wind and its neighbours by high hedges intertwined with climbing roses and honeysuckle.

The man was moved to abandon his reserve and almost to enthuse as she showed him around. She had prepared a bed for still more roses. "All one sort," she told him. "Pink ones. I do so love pink scented roses, don't you?"

Politely he agreed. "What do you feed them on?" he enquired.

"Bone meal," she told him. "And a little blood too."

The sun had appeared again, so the man sat on her small patio while she went indoors to prepare tea.

There were scones and home made fruit cake, and nice Darjeeling tea.

The man seemed more relaxed and Mrs. Mappin ventured to ask him his name. "So much more friendly, don't you think?" she said.

"Call me Jim," he said briefly.

Gently she asked him, "Are you worried, Jim?"

He looked directly at her. "I'm on the run from the police," he said.

For an instant she was disconcerted - perhaps Amy was right after all to caution her. But she soon recovered and couldn't resist asking, "Why?"

He was silent for a long moment before replying, and Mrs. Mappin was shocked when he said, quite without emotion, "I killed my wife."

It was several minutes before she could summon courage to question him further. "Why did you do it, Jim?" she asked eventually.

"She annoyed me," he said blandly, looking straight at her. "She would keep talking."

Mrs. Mappin gripped the arms of her chair and in a low voice said, "How?" In spite of herself she had to know.

He drew an implement from his pocket. It was a Stanley knife. Carefully he screwed the blade into place.

Mrs. Mappin thought it looked horribly sharp. Nervously she looked at her watch. "Perhaps it is time you were leaving," she suggested, adding "I won't tell the police you were here."

"It doesn't matter," he said, standing up and taking a step towards her. "People who talk too much annoy me."

And then it happened. Suddenly he groaned and gripped his stomach, then crumpled before her.

With relief she watched.

This evening she would plant the pink roses in their newly prepared bed, and they would have some good, new fertilizer she thought complacently. And the arsenic would help keep the weeds down too.

For Evermore

They sat beneath the high oak, its spreading arms sheltering them from the heat of the June sun. The grass was warm and the buttercups and lady's smock – tall enough to cover their legs – waved in the gentle summer breeze.

Above them a skylark trilled as it descended and rose again on strong, brown wings, high into the blue sky.

Her hair, as yellow almost as the pollen which flecked his blue trousers, was partly hidden by a bonnet, tied under her chin with pink ribbons which exactly matched her cotton frock. The full gathered skirt showed a peeping white frill of petticoat beneath.

"T'were always nice on seventh June," he remarked conversationally, running his fingers through the grass and disturbing a multitude of small insects. A fat round bumble bee, busy extracting nectar from the pink clover, buzzed loudly at the inconvenience before settling again to its task.

She nodded fondly at him. Her eyes, reflecting the blue of the sky, had a far-away look. "I'm glad we decided to meet here each year," she said softly.

He rolled the sleeves of his shirt, and the stripes twisted in the folds. "It's worth waiting for," he said placing his hand, strong, and warm from the sun, over hers.

She made a daisy-chain and hung it around his neck. "Now it's your turn," she said laughing, as his fingers fumbled with the little flowers.

For a while they were quiet, there were so many memories and most of them didn't need to be spoken. Just being there in the sunshine, their thoughts entwined, was enough.

She looked up at him seeing his dark hair glinting in the sun – just as it had used to. "You remember?" she asked.

His smile touched her heart and she knew he, too, was thinking back over the years. Seeing again the two small children playing in this meadow. Making daisy-chains to hang around each other's necks.

It had always seemed to be sunny and warm, even when they were growing up and still finding their greatest pleasure in each other's company and the countryside around them.

And then came the special year when their families and friends had filled the small church to give their blessing on the union.

"It was the seventh of June," she said aloud. "And we planted our acorn to commemorate."

"For evermore," he looked at her fondly.

Then abruptly the peace of the summer morning was shattered. Alarmed, they rose and looked in the direction of the noise. Above the hedge they could just see a large yellow object on the end of a thick rod; it was moving along in a jerky way as if whatever was carrying it found the ground uneven.

Cautiously they walked towards the hedge, the noise was louder and there was smoke and a strange smell which made her wrinkle her nose. She was frightened but their clasped hands gave her confidence.

He was able to peer above the close-knit hawthorn and they found a gap where the elder flowers and trailing honeysuckle parted so that she could see clearly.

"It's like a huge claw," he frowned in puzzlement as the yellow object dug deeply into the grassland, tossing up great wedges of soil and stones. It seemed to be propelled by the apparatus with the haze of smoke and ear-shattering noise.

She looked impishly at him. "Do you suppose it's a dragon?" she asked.

But he was unaccustomedly serious. "There are men," he said and turned away from the scene of destruction.

He helped her as she trod carefully down from the hedge so as not to crush the delicate speedwell and herb robert which, with the deep pink campion, grew in profusion amongst the starry whit-sundays and tender sweet grasses.

Her pink frock swished as they walked slowly to the far side of the field and sat again on the sun-warmed grass under the hedge which bordered the lane.

But now the peace of the beautiful day was gone. The skylark still sang, but they could no longer hear it and the gentle fragrance of summer was lost in the smoky smell.

Suddenly the noise stopped and presently men came through the gate into their field. There were four of them, and they sat with their backs to the hedge and ate and drank and afterwards spoke together in a desultory manner.

They seemed not to notice the boy and girl, even though he moved close to them so as to hear what they were saying.

After they had gone she looked anxiously up at him. "What are they doing?" she asked.

"They are going to build."

She smiled with relief. "A cottage in our meadow, that will be nice."

"No love," he looked indescribably weary, "houses. A lot of them."

For an hour or more they sat on in the sunshine, miserably knowing that this was to be the end.

The last meeting in their beloved field, the years of happiness together were over.

He held her hand as they watched the yellow machine tearing through the hedge, uprooting wild flowers and scattering birds and nestlings.

She had to shout against the noise and her face was wet with tears. "I was sorry about the baby . . ."

"Yes, I know." His voice was tender. "I couldn't let you go alone."

Sadly he looked down at her. "This must be farewell, dear. We are lucky, we have had so much happiness here."

"Yes," she sighed as the old oak tree groaned and fell. "You remember when we planted it we said it was to be for evermore."

Genius

Iain was doing his very favourite thing, sitting on the floor in the living-room writing - Mummy and Daddy called it scribbling – and at the same time listening to the words they were saying.

They talked too quickly, of course, and Iain, being 5 and a bit years old, missed a lot of words, but some he managed to scribble onto the large, fat pad Mummy had given him.

The spelling was a bit dodgy, so Daddy said, but Iain understood, and that, he thought, was what really mattered.

Most of what they were talking about was pretty dull. It seemed to Iain that something called a Fitzgerald was coming to see them. Iain didn't know who or what a Fitzgerald was, but it sounded different, and therefore interesting. He wondered if it was big like Daddy, or small and would fit comfortably into one of his toy cars. It was a big long word and would take up a lot of paper, and as it was FITZ something, that probably meant it would need a "z". There were not many words needing a "z", and that made it exciting.

He was busy pondering all this when another word caught his attention. Iain knew this was an important word because Daddy stood up to say it and his face had gone all red and he was rumpling his hair, the way he sometimes did when the next-door cat dug up seeds which he had carefully planted.

"He's impecunious!" Daddy shouted, and put a lot of expression into the word.

Iain wrote down the word carefully. His spelling, he thought, probably was a bit dodgy because, like Fitzgerald, it was a long word and he had never heard it before.

They were such exciting words and he wondered why Daddy hadn't looked pleased when he said them.

Thinking of Daddy reminded Iain of a problem which was bothering him, so he put his beautiful pad and pencil down, and went to find Daddy.

Daddy had gone into the garden, when Iain found him he was digging a nice deep hole. Iain thought it looked big enough and deep enough for a tree to live in, perhaps a holly tree which would be full of red berries which Mummy said the birds liked. Or perhaps a Christmas tree which could stay in the garden all year and have coloured lights and things on it for Father Christmas to see.

Half of Daddy was already down inside the hole and he was saying rather nasty things to the spade. His face was still red too, but that, Iain thought, was probably because he was working so hard.

Iain came straight to the point, looking down into the hole he asked: "Why is my name spelt with two 'I's' when one would be enough?"

It was a reasonable question, but just at that moment Daddy wasn't feeling reasonable.

"It's your name," he said loudly, just in case the spade couldn't hear properly. "it was your grandfather's and his father's too."

"But," Iain began, then stopped. It might be better to ask Daddy another time when he wasn't so cross with the spade.

Later that evening when Iain was safely tucked up in bed Mummy and Daddy were discussing the events of the day. They supposed their good-for-nothing nephew would come in the morning and stay for lunch.

"I suppose we shall have to feed him" Daddy said uncharitably.

"Perhaps he will have changed, improved" Mummy said hopefully. "Do you think a salad would be all right for lunch?"

In Daddy's opinion all food – at any time – would be wasted on Fitzgerald. With a sudden change of interest Daddy exclaimed, "Do you know what Iain asked me today? He wanted to know why there are two "I's" in his name!"

"Oh I've always wondered about that," Mummy said. "Why are there?"

Daddy stared at her as if astonished at such ignorance. "It's hereditary," he said as if that explained everything.

Mummy looked puzzled. "Your name is Owen" she said. "Is that hereditary too?" When Daddy didn't answer she added: "Iain has a wonderful way with words. Spelling too," she added.

"He can't do sums or – or geography," Daddy pointed out.

"He's only five years old!" Mummy protested. "When I spoke with his teacher today she said he would learn to do those things – and she said that he was a genius with writing and spelling."

"A genius," Daddy repeated. "Well, not every family has one of those. And only five years old too!" He was smiling and suggested an early night so as to have strength for their visitor tomorrow. "A genius," he repeated softly to himself on his way upstairs. Well, perhaps arithmetic and geography were not all that important when one was five years old. Maybe tomorrow he would make a point of discussing that extra "I" with his clever son.

It was eleven o'clock next morning when the car drew up alongside their house. Daddy, looking through the window, gave a low whistle.

"Come and look at this, dear," he called to Mummy. "That'll make the neighbours talk!"

Iain looked too. The car was long and low and bright shining red. A Porsche, Daddy said. Iain following them out to greet their guest and wondered how Porsche should be spelt.

"Come and meet your cousin," Mummy said. "Fitzgerald, this is Iain."

So that's what a Fitzgerald is, Iain thought and mentally crossed the word off his beautiful pad.

Fitzgerald said a casual "Hallo little man," without really looking down at Iain. He was not as tall as Daddy, Iain noticed, and he hadn't shaved properly. He had two thin stripes of dark hair on his upper lip. He was busy now showing Daddy things about the car: how the gears worked - and if you pushed this, the roof opened or shut.

Mummy was on the other side of the car talking to a lady. "Iain, dear," she called "come and help Dorinda out of the car."

Iain held the door open for her. Dorinda flicked dark curls from her shoulders and glanced down at him, but he thought that she didn't really see him because her eyes had dark shadows around them, the way Daddy's had when he'd "walked into a lamppost" as Mummy said, some weeks ago. Her eyelashes were long and thick too. So he was not surprised when she couldn't see his hand, offering to help her out of the car.

He watched as she gently tested the hard driveway with one foot before allowing the other foot to follow.

Iain was fascinated to watch her. Mummy got out of their car quickly. Of course it wasn't long and low like this one, and this lady hadn't got her arms full of potatoes and cabbages and things, which probably made a difference.

Dorinda's shoes interested him too, he wondered how they stayed on with such thin straps and with heels that looked like the long nails that Daddy had knocked into one of their fence posts a few weeks ago - only longer of course.

He looked at the lady with admiration as she adjusted her red skirt – thought there wasn't a lot of it, and wound a long, red scarf around her neck. He made a note that when his knees got cold he would put a scarf around his own neck.

Indoors Iain was sitting in his usual place on the floor, his pad and pencil were ready, and he was trying to remember the lovely long word Daddy had spoken yesterday. He had written it down, the trouble was remembering how it sounded.

Daddy was busy talking to Fitzgerald. "What exactly is your occupation now?" Daddy asked.

Iain noticed that Daddy hadn't mentioned 'work', just 'occupation'.

"Well," said Fitzgerald, and put his coffee cup down on the table by his chair so as to have two hands free. "I have several irons in the fire at the moment," he said casually and waved his arms in a sort of "free" and nonchalant way. "At the moment I'm considering an offer from Hemmingway which is quite attractive, and the racing people have my name high in their books."

"So what are you doing right now?" Daddy said. "That car must cost a pretty penny to run."

"Oh! I've not *bought* the car!" Fitzgerald laughingly assured Daddy. "This is just a trial run. I'll find something wrong with it, so they probably won't charge at all for this day."

Iain noticed that Daddy's face was getting red again.

"You mean," said Daddy loudly "you are out of work, and – and driving a Porsche?"

"I wouldn't have put it that way," Fitzgerald protested. "Just between jobs."

Suddenly it came to Iain, the word he had been puzzling over. "He's Impecunious" he shouted, pleased to have remembered such a long and important-sounding word.

Fitzgerald and Dorinda left without finishing their coffee. The engine of the Porsche leapt into action and Dorinda's red scarf billowed out behind her as they sped down the road.

Daddy and Mummy were holding hands when they came back into the room.

"You see," said Mummy, looking fondly down at their son. "He is a genius."

Any Old Car In A Storm

Robert's car ran out of petrol on the way home. At first I didn't believe him. At a quarter to twelve, on a bitingly cold night, on an unlit road? It was the sort of thing that only happened in movies. Horror movies.

Robert was worried, apologetic too, but mostly worried. "I'm sorry, Jo," he said and I could see he was; the nervous twitch at the corner of his mouth was winking away as it always did when something bothered him. "I wouldn't have had this happen for anything in the world," he said.

"It didn't need 'anything,'" I replied tartly. "Just a fill-up with petrol before we started out."

"I filled her up on Wednesday."

"This," I pointed out, "is Sunday."

"But I haven't been anywhere - much - since then. Do you think she's using too much petrol?" The twitch was working overtime now.

"At the moment, that is quite immaterial," I said. "What matters now, is how am I to get home - it is at least a mile."

"I know," he said miserably. "I'm sorry Jo, I really am. Do you think you could phone the all-night garage when you get back? Ask them to bring some petrol out for me?"

I glared at him unbelievingly. "You mean you are going to let me walk back on my own, in the dark – on this lonely road?"

"I can't leave the car, Jo, you must see that I can't. Anything could happen to it, someone could steal it. . ."

"It hasn't any petrol." I was trying hard to keep my temper.

"No - well they might have some in a can. Or they might pinch the wheels or something. It's a valuable car, Jo!" Robert said pathetically.

"And I'm not?" I was furious now. For the moment, much too angry to be frightened about the walk home - or bothered because my shoes were just straps on spindly heels, and my dress flimsy black chiffon with only a shawl to cover it.

I opened the car door and stepped out into the darkness, the wind seared through me as if I wasn't in its way at all.

"Goodbye," I shouted and the wind blew the words back into my face. I leaned into the car so that Robert would be certain to hear what I said. "If I get back safely," I screamed, emphasising the 'if', "I will telephone the garage and tell them that you let me walk home alone."

"Jo," I heard him call before I slammed the door.

I strode off into the night. It was very dramatic, but it didn't stay that way. The sandals and dress which had been perfect for a dinner party, were no match for the rutted road and force nine northerly gale.

It didn't take long for my bravado to wear off. I leant into the wind and it pushed back hard so that my every step was twice the effort. I lost count of the times I tripped and almost fell in unseen bumps and ruts. The night was black as my dress - only it wasn't see-through like chiffon. My hair, which had taken hours to arrange for the party, whirled round my head and blew strands in my eyes.

Trees which bordered the road creaked and tossed in the wind, flinging down twigs and branches as if in obeisance to the storm.

Noise filled the night, it would have hidden any other sound; a wild boar could have squealed, a lion could have roared, a marauding male could have stamped his feet as he approached and I wouldn't have been able to distinguish the sound.

I have never been so scared. To keep my spirits up I concentrated hard on hating Robert and the valuable, antique automobile which took up so much of his time and affection.

Why did he have to be the one to live next door to us? Why, since we were children, did our parents assume we'd end up by marrying? It was ridiculous. I was fond of Robert - like a brother - but he was infuriating. Even as a child he'd always been absorbed in taking his latest toy to pieces when I wanted him to climb trees, and bicycling with him was no fun at all because we had to stop so often for him to adjust a screw or take off the chain or something.

Now, at eighteen, I'd had enough; I didn't intend to play second fiddle to any more machinery.

I kept peering around in case someone was following me though, goodness knows, it would have been difficult to see anyone in that inky darkness and impossible to hear. By the time I staggered up our garden path I was exhausted and chilled right through.

With fingers too cold to feel I fumbled in my black satin evening bag for the house keys, thanking goodness that the bag hung on my arm by its gilt chain - else I would surely have lost it.

Finding the locks was another problem and turning the keys in them needed all my remaining strength.

I was feeling sorry for myself now. I shouldn't have bothered to be quiet. I should have hammered on the door and roused my parents. Awakened them from their cosy slumber. They would have gone to bed early, content in the knowledge that Robert was taking care of their beloved daughter and assured that he would see me safely home, as he had so many times before.

It was warm in the house. I went into the kitchen and made myself a hot drink and filled a bottle, cuddling it in an effort to stop myself shivering. Then I went upstairs, turned on the tap and drew a warm bath.

I poured in a lot of my precious bath oil - this was not a time to be stingy. Lying in the warm, scented water I let the comfort of it seep through me.

I was luxuriating in it when I remembered Robert. By now he, too, was probably stiff with cold, part of the metal and leather monster. Frozen and quite literally attached to it.

I giggled at the thought - and then immediately was conscience-striken. Poor Robert, he would be hating himself – as well as being cold.

I wrapped the bath towel around me and went to get the phone, then back again in the scented warmth, I spoke to the man at the garage.

"Can you take a can of petrol out to..." I started.

"Sorry lady," a gruff voice answered. "I'm on my own, can't leave the premises."

"But he's stuck out there, miles from civilisation," I exaggerated a bit. "And probably frozen too."

"Bad luck," remarked the voice on the phone.

"And a tree might have fallen on him," I added for good measure.

"In that case I couldn't get to him anyway," said the man.

"You really mean you won't do it?"

"I really mean it. Good night lady."

There was a click as the receiver was replaced.

I lay back fuming. "Of all the lousy things. We'll never get petrol from him again," I told the phone.

Poor Robert, out there in the storm. A tree might really have fallen on him. He could, by now, be a squashy mess in the tangled wreckage of his beloved car.

There was only one thing for it. Jo to the rescue, I thought.

Galvanised into action, I dried myself quickly and piled on all the woollies I could lay hands on. Covering the lot with my father's anorak, I grabbed his car keys and sallied forth into the storm again.

It hadn't eased at all; the trees still waved wildly and tore at me as I got into the car. They buffeted me on all sides and threw debris against the windscreen making the short journey as hazardous as they could.

Robert was still there; he climbed stiffly out of his car as I approached. I could see he was as frozen as I had been.

"Jo," he called, "I've been so worried, cursing myself for letting you go alone. You're all right, are you?"

"Yes," I said. "The garage man wouldn't come."

"So you came instead. I don't deserve it, Jo."

"No," I agreed, lifting the spare can of petrol from the boot. My father is a methodical man and always carried some with him - and a rope, just in case.

Robert's hands were too cold, so I poured the petrol into his tank and started the engine for him. He stood there in the road, his dark hair - always unruly - blowing wildly in the wind.

"Jo," he shouted against the storm, "I'll never forgive myself."

"I know," I shouted back. "Let's go home and have a hot drink, then you can apologise properly."

With difficulty I reversed the car in the narrow road and we started off slowly in convoy. Suddenly there was an almighty crash ahead of us as a giant beech succumbed to the storm.

We climbed out and stood looking at it. A few yards farther and. . . well, it didn't bear thinking of.

Shakily I clung to Robert. "That was a close thing," I whispered in his ear.

He held me tight. "And all because of me and that damned car!"

Quickly he released me and turned and kicked the car - hard. His car. His precious car. It was difficult to credit. I gaped at him.

Well, I thought, when I'd got my breath back. Now we know what to be doing next weekend. It will be spent making good any damage he's done.

"I'll get rid of it," Robert shouted. "I'll sell it - or give it away."

"No you won't," I shouted back. "I haven't gone through all this trauma just for you to get rid of the car. You'll look after it and... and fill it up with petrol."

It was too dark to see the expression on Robert's face. We got in the back of my father's car and cuddled closely to keep warm while the trees threw branches on top of us.

"I don't want to complain," Robert said tentatively after a few minutes. "But there is something hard digging into my side."

I felt in the pocket of the anorak. There was a flask. In triumph I brought it out. My father is not only methodical, he is prepared for emergencies too.

We shared the contents of the flask, and forgot about the storm and being marooned and the danger.

Perhaps, I thought as we snuggled together, just perhaps my parents were right after all.

Gertie And The Face

I was surprised to see the wallflowers - always there had been polyanthus on the strip leading up to the green front door. The same sort of colour, of course, I told myself pausing to tap my pipe out on the gate - but Bobby always planted polyanthus.

From the flowers, my gaze rested - if that is the right word - on the door; it was red - a bright, shrieking red that somehow managed to clash with all the wallflowers.

Bobby must have gone mad, I thought, or colour blind.

And then another thought struck me. Perhaps Bobby was no longer there, perhaps. . .

Scent from the wallflowers wafted across as I strode up the path; it had been only three months since I'd heard from Bobby. Bobby's letters were written four times a year, quarterly without fail. The contents were pretty stereotyped too and his last letter had been no exception. "How are you? I'm well apart from my indigestion. Gertie's well apart from her arthritis. The lads at the Crown and Anchor send their compliments. Well, Cheerio, Bobby." Not what you could call newsy, but at least it was a link.

I pressed the bell and a moment later the red front door opened a few inches. The face I glimpsed wasn't Gertie's.

"Excuse me," I said. "Is Bobby at home?"

The door opened a fraction more. "No," said the face which wasn't Gertie's.

It was a brief, uncompromising remark and the face didn't smile.

She was about to close the door again when I said, "I'm an old friend of his, I was just passing..."

The face, now fully revealed, glared at me owlishly through round, gold-framed spectacles.

"I haven't seen him for several years," I added, "and his last letter. . ."

There was a slight change of expression on the face. "He writes to you?" it said.

"Every three months," I offered.

She nodded and opened the door wider. "Well, you'd better come in."

It was hardly welcoming but I followed her into the familiar front room - only it wasn't familiar. Gone were the friendly, worn plush arm chairs, the sporting pictures around the walls and the smell of stale tobacco. Instead the room was bright with chintzes, flower prints were on the walls and it all smelled of polish and disinfectant.

The face sat itself cautiously in one of the gaudy chairs and, with the wave of a hand, indicated another opposite. Gingerly I perched on the edge of it, memories of sinking comfortably into worn green plush flashed across my mind.

"Bobby," I said, "is he all right?"

"Yes, he's at his office."

"Office?" I queried. Bobby worked with the other lads at a bench handling tools. A manual, man's job. Not in an office.

"At his office," she repeated the words slowly, spelling them out so that illiterates like me could understand.

There was an uneasy silence while I tried to think of something else to say. Then, "When will he be home?" I asked.

The gold-framed eyes focussed on a gilt, star shaped clock poised on the wall between a picture of rampant columbines and miniature pansies and another of stylized white daisies leaning perilously out of a hideous red tub.

"Half past five," she said.

Following her gaze I looked at the clock; it was just four. There didn't seem to be much chance of a cup of tea - leave alone a slice of cake; it might make crumbs on the floor, I thought uncharitably.

I stood up. "I'll be going," I said.

She beat me to the door and didn't bother to say goodbye.

I strolled up the road towards the factory where Bobby had his 'office'. There were things I had to know and the only means of finding out was to waylay Bobby when he left his place of work.

There was time to spare so I called in at the Crown and Anchor. With relief I found that it looked the same as when I moved away.

Joe was there behind the bar and his cheerful grin was as warming as the foaming glass he handed me. "Good to see you lad!" he said, and sounded as if he really meant it.

There weren't many customers in the bar so I was able to answer questions about my job in the North.

"It isn't at all grotty," I told him, remembering remarks the lads had made when I set off for such foreign parts. "Wigan is a good place to live."

"I've heard the pier's nice," Joe said, and added "We still miss you down here."

"Seen Bobby lately?" I asked casually.

Joe sucked in his breath. "Doesn't come in much now."

"No?"

"No," he replied. "Not since..."

"Since what?"

"Excuse me a moment," Joe apologised - busily filling glasses for new customers.

It was fifteen minutes and another pint before he returned. I repeated my question.

"Thing is," said Joe. "Since Gertie cracked up..."

"What do you mean 'cracked up'?"

"Well, her arthritis, you know."

"I know she had arthritis, she always did." I hadn't meant it to sound unfeeling, callous. It just came out that way. "Gertie's salt of the earth," I added, making amends.

Joe looked at me strangely. "I know," he said.

He was off again dealing with other customers. Joe was always a good host but his conversation was somewhat restricted.

I edged my way out of the pub and headed towards the factory. There was still a bit of time to go but it was interesting to see the changes three years had brought. The factory, for a start. It looked quite new, rebuilt, and the name on the outside was different too.

I whistled under my breath: you couldn't leave anything. Perhaps Bobby really did work in an office now. Why hadn't he mentioned these things when he wrote? I already knew about his indigestion and Gertie's arthritis.

Promptly at 5:30 the first trickle of workers came through the gates, then the flood and last of all Bobby. He didn't seem to be in a hurry. There was no marked enthusiasm for getting home quickly. Not like the old days, hurrying to get back to Gertie.

"Hello Old Pal," I said as he came alongside.

He stopped dead, eyes nearly popping out. "Gawd," he said. "It's Jack."

"Right first time."

Bobby just stood there, staring, so I said, "You on your way home? Can we talk somewhere?"

In the old days I'd have just gone with him and Gertie would have found me something to eat. Sausages or something, it never seemed to be a problem for her - except, of course, carrying things about – and we did that. All easy and friendly. Perhaps we'd taken it too much for granted, I thought.

"Er, well," Bobby hesitated. "You see Sylvia . . ."

So the face had a name. Sylvia didn't seem appropriate. But then I was biased.

"After you've eaten?" I suggested. "At the Crown and Anchor?"

"Well," he said again. "Sylvia doesn't like me going there. But tell you what," he brightened - almost smiled like the old Bobby. "I'll meet you up the road at seven. We'll go and see Gertie."

I watched him heading towards his colourful, antiseptic home and tried to imagine the greeting Sylvia would have prepared. It obviously wasn't worth hurrying for.

I found a pizza place and sat there eating and thinking about Bobby and Gertie, and wondering what the hell Sylvia was up to, and how on earth she'd managed to reduce Bobby to such a shadow of a man. A mouse-like Bobby, instead of a secure, confident Robert.

At seven o'clock I was poised around the corner of the road, out of sight in case Sylvia was on guard. A couple of minutes later Bobby came steaming along, red in the face, and belligerent.

"She didn't want me to come," he said when he'd got his breath back. "She said it wasn't Wednesday so what was I doing, seeing Gertie today." He glared at me as if I was the one trying to stop him.

"I told her," he went on, "I didn't care if it was Christmas Day, I wanted to see Gertie and that was where I was going."

"Quite right too."

We were sitting in the bus when he told me how Gertie had fallen and broken her hip. "When she came home from hospital my cousin Sylvia offered to come. Just to help out, you know."

"And stayed?" I said.

He nodded. "After a week or so she said it was too much for her, looking after Gertie and the house. Said her heart was bad."

"So Gertie went into a home?" I queried.

"Yes, it was to be for a few weeks, but Sylvia always had a reason why it had to be longer and in the meantime she was changing things at home. I should have been firmer," he said miserably. "But at the time . . ."

"Understandable," I murmured.

He looked at me gratefully. "Thanks, Jack," he said. "I'm glad you came, you're good for me."

And bad for Sylvia, I hoped.

Gertie was walking with the aid of a frame. "I'm getting on," she said. "Soon be home."

I gave her a bunch of polyanthus I'd bought. She smiled, burying her nose in them. "How lovely. Reminds me of our garden."

Bobby looked at me, squaring his shoulders as if preparing for future battle.

* * *

I arranged to meet Bobby next evening at the Crown and Anchor. "Seven o'clock sharp," I reminded him as we parted. "And to blazes with Sylvia."

He was there at seven too. "I don't understand," he confided, wiping the froth from his chin. "She was nice as pie. The pie was nice too," he reminisced. "Steak and kidney."

"Never mind the pie," I said. "Did you tell her?"

"Told her last night," said Bobby. "Sylvia", I said, "Gertie's coming home on Friday."

"What did she say?"

"She just looked - then asked if I'd be home to supper. She's never done that before."

"She's trying to get around you," I warned. "Don't you be fooled."

"I won't," Bobby said. "I want my Gertie home."

Our next meeting in the Crown and Anchor was to report on arrangements for Gertie's homecoming. Neighbours had been alerted and willingly offered help on a rota system. The doctor had been told and there was even a hint of meals-on-wheels.

"Everyone loves Gertie," I told Bobby as I quaffed a well-earned pint.

"Not surprised," he said.

"How's the gorgon?" I asked.

"Still as nice as pie!"

Bobby looked puzzled. "Funny thing," he mused. "It's as if the wind's gone out of her sails. She's docile, waits for me to tell her, instead of ordering me about."

"My influence," I grinned. "I should have come before."

He ignored that. "I told her you were having supper with us tomorrow."

"Oh no!" I exclaimed. An evening with the face - even if it was docile - was not on my itinerary.

"You're coming," said Bobby. And I could see how - at last - he'd managed to subdue Sylvia.

The next evening I took care dressing for my visit, chiefly, I told myself, because Gertie's homecoming was a special occasion. But partly because it took up time. Time which I didn't want to spend in company with Sylvia.

I dawdled up the path beside the wallflowers and pressed the bell. My face cracked into what I hoped was a grin when she opened the door. Faithful to tradition there was no answering smile.

The meal couldn't have been better. Strange, I thought, how someone with a sour expression could produce such edible food.

It was touching to see Gertie and Bobby so happy together again.

After we'd eaten I went into the kitchen to help the face with the washing up; she didn't speak at all and it wasn't till after we'd finished that I noticed she'd been quietly crying. Slow moving tears trickled down her cheeks.

I couldn't just walk away so, embarrassed, I gave her my handkerchief and said "Would you like to come out for a drink? We could leave the lovebirds alone for a while."

I was surprised - well, appalled - when she nodded.

We went to the Crown and Anchor and as we entered Joe hid his grin behind a large, beery hand. Sylvia drank a whisky-mac, and loosened up a bit.

"You see," she said and sounded almost human, "I sold my house after I came here. It was wrong but I wanted this to be my home. I can't stay now - anyway Bobby good as told me to go."

She started weeping again and her glasses got all wet. I got her another whisky - and another for myself while I was about it.

"I've nowhere to go," Sylvia said, and managed to look pathetic. I handed her my second-best handkerchief.

"How long are you staying?" she asked in a voice wet with tears and whisky.

"Me? Oh, I go home tomorrow."

"Where is home?"

"Wigan," I said. "It's a good place, not grotty at all." And wondered muzzily where I'd heard that before.

"I've never been to Wigan," Sylvia said.

Visions of the dinner, still warm inside me, floated before my eyes. Roast beef, all red in the middle, Yorkshire pudding just as it should be with a small puddle of gravy on it - followed by superb, melting pastry on the apple pie.

The way to a man's heart, I thought. Well, perhaps not his heart - just his inner being.

Critically I looked across the table at her. For a start she'd have to change those gold-rimmed specs.

"I quite like wallflowers," I said.

Pink And Blue And Yellow And Green

The wild flowers grew in profusion; daisies tall, and oxeye, the sort that are said to brighten Scottish homes through the month of June.

Mingled with them, pink clover and yellow buttercups peered above the grass, and speedwell reflected the blue of a cloudless sky where the brown lark trilled, far above its nestlings.

A considerate, or just an observant person, might have hesitated even to tiptoe across the meadow for fear of harming such delicate beauty. But many people see only what they want to and some can only appreciate ordered uniformity.

To the farmer the meadow spoke of danger for his cattle from the shining, golden buttercups which, if grazed on inadvertently, would surely cause stomach upsets - with consequent loss of his income.

The buttercup roots, too, were strong and resilient, and would be difficult to remove.

The tenacious fragility of the speedwell filled the farmer with gloom since its being there proved that the lime-hating crop he had planned for the meadow next year would not thrive. So all his scheme of rotation would need to be reviewed.

The beauty of the clover, too, brought him no answering joy. The large pink flowers were useless to his busy hives of honey bees who could not reach the nectar contained in each floret.

Had they been simple, small white clover he would have eyed them with contentment, safe in the knowledge that his bees would be working hard to fill their supers before the crop was harvested for winter cattle feed.

The daisies were, to him, the final blot on his landscape – serving no useful purpose at all.

Leaning sun browned arms on the top of his gate, he pondered the hard work ahead. Ploughing, tilling, fertilizing, spraying all those weeds.

Then perhaps, God willing, next year he would be looking on a field of corn. Not yet golden, but strong and uniformly maturing. Perhaps, also, that lark singing so lustily overhead would have the grace to raise its young in someone else's pasture.

Through narrowed eyes the farmer watched a young couple across the field. They should be in Sunday School, he thought, not playing about in his meadow.

The boy and girl were too absorbed with each other to notice the farmer.

Joyfully they ran on the sweet smelling grass.

"I'll spread a carpet for you to walk on," said the boy.

She laughed and the sound wafted high on the summer breeze and mingled with the song of the skylark. "What colour will it be?" she asked.

"Pink and blue and yellow and green," he said, spreading his arms as though he was indeed laying all the beauty just for her.

He was surprised that such words should come from him; short months ago he would have jeered had anyone suggested he could behave in this way.

He watched, entranced as she minced on the carpet he had lain for her, and laughed as she curtsied her thanks to him.

They held hands and danced on the warm summer grass, with no thought for the bruised flowers which followed their every step.

When they tired she flung herself onto the grass and looked up at him, smiling her welcome.

He gathered flowers in each of his capable hands and pulled them apart, dropping them lovingly over her.

"Confetti," he said.

And they lay together in the sunshine while the lark trilled anxiously overhead.

Gamblers Eponymous

The rain started just before they reached the café, big thundery drops which plopped onto the plastic bags and made damp, widening circles on Sarah's blue cotton frock.

"Bet you a fiver it stops before we come out," Sarah predicted breathlessly.

"You really mustn't bet. It's a waste of money!" Emily turned up the collar of her mackintosh and ran towards the café. She pushed at the door and held it open while Sarah edged her way in, her assortment of well-filled string and plastic carriers bouncing off the frames.

There was a free table at the far end of the room, and Sarah jostled her ample form in and out of the tables, seemingly unaware of – and certainly untroubled by – the glares and cutting remarks which followed her progress.

Embarrassed for her friend, Emily followed at a slight distance, trying to look unconcerned and as if she had no connection with the nuisance ahead. Her own basket was of a size large enough to carry all her immediate needs, but not so big that it bumped into other shoppers. She settled herself and stowed it neatly under the table by her feet, well out of the way, when the waitress brought their coffee and toasted tea-cakes.

Sarah distributed her packages and bags with a careless abandon: they settled in untidy heaps on the vacant chair beside her and overflowed on to the territory of the next door table, the occupants of which stared meaningfully and uttered, *sotto voce*, remarks similar to those which had followed Sarah's progress up the room. Unconcerned, she shovelled demerara sugar liberally into her cup and took a deep gulp. "I was ready for that!" she beamed across the table at her friend.

"It is refreshing," Emily agreed.

Sarah concentrated her energies on the tea-cake. "Tiring work, shopping," she said after a moment, her mouth managing to cope with the words and the bun at the same time.

Emily looked away from her, down at her own plate and swallowed hard before answering - as if, by doing so herself, she could somehow force Sarah not to talk with her own mouth full in future.

It wouldn't work that way, of course. How many years had she known Sarah? Thirty or forty at least, and she had always spoken with her mouth full. If she hadn't known Sarah so well, Emily would have thought she did it just to annoy.

"Oh, that was good." Sarah gave a great sigh of repletion and pushed a flabby hand through short, grey hair. "Finished your shopping?" she queried.

Emily nodded, her mouth being occupied by tea-cake. Sarah glanced around at her assorted packages. "Don't know how you manage on such a tiny amount," she commented cheerfully. "I seem to get a small mountain of stuff each week."

"You eat more," Emily said tartly.

Sarah laughed and her frame wobbled in rhythm. "That follows," she said. "How about seeing a film before we go home?"

"What's on?" Emily was torn between the desire to see a 'good' film and the trauma of coping with Sarah and her shopping at the cinema.

"Dunno, but we can see." She ferreted amongst her purchases, scattering things around the table and floor until her copy of the local paper emerged. She spread it over the table on top of everything and searched for the entertainment page.

"H'm, not very promising. A couple of horrors and a Top Cat," she said eventually.

"We'd better go straight home I suppose." Emily knew that relief was uppermost.

"I want to put something on False Start, then I'm ready." Sarah began to collect all her belongings together; the newspaper first, scrumpled into the bottom of a carrier bag advertising Puffer Corn in bold red letters, on top of it tumbled onions, cream, shoe polish and tooth paste.

Emily winced as she watched her friend's method of packing. "I wish you wouldn't waste your money on horses," she protested.

Sarah was picking things up from the floor. "It's only fifty pence each way – and it's fun. Besides, I might win!"

"I don't hold with gambling." Emily hoped she didn't sound too prim.

"You don't even hold with church raffles!" Sarah grinned across the table. "Come on, have a go. 'If you don't speculate you can't accumulate'. Put a couple of bob on False Start and we'll share the proceeds!"

"If I were to bet – and I'm not going to – I certainly wouldn't choose a horse with that name."

Sarah heaved herself up onto her feet and gathered the bags around her ample frame. "There are other horses and other names – but I know how you feel about gambling. You wait outside while I nip in and offer them my hard-won pennies."

As Sarah had prophesied, it had stopped raining. Emily waited a little distance from the betting shop, clutching her basket and standing guard over the assorted shopping bags ranged around her on the pavement. 'I look as if I'm expecting the dustman to call', she thought unhappily.

Sarah had a seat to herself on the bus. There wasn't room for both of them and the packages. Getting on and off was a squeeze too, and Emily had to retrieve several oranges which escaped from Sarah's bags and rolled under the seats.

The bus stop was nearby, but they were both glad when they reached home. Sarah's house was first, with the front gate propped permanently open.

"Unlock the door for me," she said. "You'll find the key in my pocket. Save me putting this lot down."

Emily felt in the proffered pocket and walked up the short path between rows of overgrown roses and trailing honeysuckle. Canterbury bells and sweet williams jostled marigolds and asters – and mixed with them all was a plentiful supply of wild flowers.

"Thanks, love," said Sarah, pushing her way into the hall. 'I'll see you later,' she called to the retreating figure. "I'll bring in the winnings and we'll celebrate!"

Her fat, cheerful laugh followed Emily up her own neat garden path. The other half of the semi was quite different, the paintwork shining and the grass properly manicured.

Emily took her basket into the kitchen and carefully stowed away the shopping. Then in the quiet of her tidy, polished home she settled down to fill in her football pools.

Pictures In The Mind

Ben stood smiling absently in the summer sunshine – what remained of his white, woolly hair blowing in the soft breeze.

"Did I ever tell you about Bill Smith?" he said.

I brushed a marauding fly from the end of my nose and squinted lazily up at the sun. It was pleasant lying on the warm grass; in my opinion a proper way to enjoy well-earned retirement. "Which Bill Smith?" I asked, not really wanting to know.

"William Smith Esq., late of fifty-three Wentworth Drive."

I opened both eyes then and looked suspiciously up at Ben. "That's my address."

He grinned smugly and nodded, satisfied that my attention was aroused and focussed on him.

"Well, what about him?" I asked grudgingly.

He leaned down and plucked a juicy blade of grass and inspected it minutely before inserting the stem into his mouth, then he lowered himself gingerly beside me and took time arranging his hands comfortably behind his head.

Ben can be maddeningly slow at times, and he just gets worse if you try to hurry him.

"Well, what about this William Smith?" I chivvied again; it seemed minutes since Ben had settled himself on the grass and I was afraid he had already fallen asleep.

He gave a little jerk before replying, confirming my suspicion. "Well," he said, taking his time about it. "He committed suicide, you know."

He knew I didn't know. "Where?" Pictures of the rooms in my home chased one another through my mind. Had he attempted it in the kitchen? Perhaps he'd been driven to the very depths of despair in our bedroom. Or in the potting shed at the end of our garden where I spent many happy hours.

"Where? Oh he strung himself up somewhere I believe," Ben said, and after a moment's thought added "used an old tie, a real silk one so I heard. They had to throw it away - no one felt like putting it around his own neck afterwards. A waste really." He turned a bland face towards me.

I shivered in spite of the warm sunshine. We'd lived in number fifty-three for ten years now – going on eleven – and it was a happy house. Well, we'd always thought it was.

But the knowledge that someone there had been desperately unhappy was chilling. Perhaps there were ghosts and, what were they called? Yes, bad vibes, of which, so far, we'd been unaware.

"But where?" I repeated. "Which room?" It was horrifying, but I had to know.

"Oh," he was silent for what seemed like an eternity – lying there, one large hand shielding his eyes from the bright sunlight. "Now I remember," he said at last. "The kitchen. Tied himself up to one of the cupboard handles. The top ones."

I nodded, it would have to be. They were high enough for a really determined man to dangle from.

It was disturbing and I spared a thought for the poor soul who found him.

"Terrible for his wife – she discovered him I suppose."

"No, she'd gone already. It was because of that he did it. Couldn't face life without her you see."

I did see only too well, and I could sympathise too. If anything were to happen to Janet . . . I pushed the thought to the back of my mind. Other more immediate problems needed consideration.

We were happy living at number fifty-three; we had friends, and the family were near – but not too near. It was convenient in all ways and we'd planned to grow old there. 'Mature' Janet called it, though goodness knows we were that already.

I blanched at the upheaval of moving, Janet would hate it too. And how could I explain to her that we needed to move? She was highly-strung, 'nervy' the doctor said – whatever that meant.

When we had first decided to live there, Janet had stipulated a newish house 'so that I can be sure no-one has died in the bedrooms'. She'd have hysterics if I told her that not only had someone done just that – and probably in our master bedroom, but that a body had dangled from the kitchen cupboard as well.

The answer, of course, was not to tell her; to go on living there as before – but I'm sensitive too and, to tell the truth, a bit squeamish as well.

I knew I'd never again go into the kitchen without visualising the dangling shape, grotesquely swinging. The bedroom would seem different too, not so cosy.

No, we must move. I'd have to think up some good reason to satisfy Janet. Dry rot or woodworm, or an infestation of mice. She didn't like them either.

Ben had gone right off to sleep. I gave him a prod, I didn't see why he should doze there peacefully in the sunshine when he'd stirred up such a hornets' nest.

"Feel like a drink?" he said.

"I could use one," I said fervently.

We got stiffly to our feet and strolled past the pond where children were paddling and sailing their boats. It was our favourite walk, especially on a warm day like this, and I knew I'd miss it when we moved.

Slowly we strolled down the hill, pausing as we always did to admire the view across the valley. It didn't seem right that, amid such beauty people could be so unhappy they were prepared to end it all.

I knew I was being naïve, stupid too, but Ben's story had really upset me. And it was our house which was involved.

The morning didn't seem nearly as bright and warm as it had. I even dreaded the prospect of going home to Janet! Something I'd never imagined happening.

I glanced at Ben – he was smiling to himself. Because of the day, I wondered, the warmth and the sunshine? Or because he had hoodwinked me with one of his tall stories?

Usually I laughed at them, but this one wasn't funny from any angle – especially mine.

"This William Smith," I reminded him. "Did he live at fifty-three for long?" He stopped smiling then and considered, rubbing his nose with a forefinger. "Not long, his only son went up North to live. Rotherham or somewhere like that."

"So?" I prompted, trying to cast aside the mental picture of the late W. Smith dangling perhaps for days before being discovered.

He gave me a crafty, sidelong look. "They moved up there to be near him, you see. It was sometime before we heard what happened to them. Your turn to buy the drinks," he said.

Like April

It was just getting dusk on an Autumn evening – the eve of All Saints as it happened, though I hadn't thought about it at the time - when a sudden squall nearly stopped me in my tracks; the wind fierce, like a living thing hurling itself at me, flinging great icy drops of rain into my face.

I should have noticed the dark, looming cloud but the street lights were on and they always seem to hide the sky, and anyway the pavement was rough where the roots from the senescent oaks had disturbed the tarmac - so my eyes were concerned with them rather than what was going on up above.

I dodged as a figure came towards me on the narrow pavement; headlamps from slow-moving cars lit up the shafts of rain like firework sparklers as we passed.

"What a shower!" I gasped.

"Like April," she replied.

It was a musical voice, lilting, haunting, enchanting. I hadn't seen her face, she'd been just a dark shape amongst the sparkling raindrops.

'Like April,' I repeated her words softly to myself, but they didn't sound the same when I said them.

I had half a mind to run and follow her; to see her again, to find out where she went, who she was. But in that rain? It would be crazy!

So I walked on, the water now seeping into my shoes and dripping in a steady flow down the back of my neck. Cars sloshed more water but I was wet enough not to notice.

Another figure appeared through the rain; not hurrying, just drifting along with shining, dark clothes which billowed in the wind.

I saw her face quite clearly as she passed beneath a street lamp. She was smiling, serene, beautiful.

"It's like April!" she said as she passed me.

I stopped and turned to watch her but the wind blew more rain into my eyes and she had gone when I opened them again.

"You're dreaming," I said aloud and pinched myself sharply. It hurt.

"You're not dreaming." The voice was soft, inviting. It seemed to come from above now, mingled with branches of the oak trees.

'It's just the rustle of leaves - and your imagination,' I told myself. But all the same I stood and peered up into the tree; its branches were tossing and swaying; leaves which had been clinging desperately now flew in wild circles. In the noise and hustle it was easy to imagine anything.

As suddenly as it had started, the rain ceased and the wind shrank to a gentle breeze. I was still looking up into the tree; there was fluttering and movement in the dark depths; perhaps the branches and leaves settling into more regular positions, but a sound like a whisper, a sigh, murmured, 'You see, just like April.'

A shining new moon emerged between streaming clouds and through the tangled branches I saw a black shape etched against its brightness.

A cat? An owl? I couldn't be sure.

I splashed on down the road again; someone was coming towards me, clearly visible in the light from the moon. Tall, angular, her rain hat whipped to a point by the wind and glistening wet, the light playing queer tricks with shadows on her face, making her nose appear long and curved.

She carried an umbrella - blown inside-out by the squall, but she smiled a strange grin.

Her voice was a harsh, grating croak: "Just like April isn't it?" she said as she passed me by.

I walked on, remembering it was Halloween, and wondering.

Quercus

Phillida came to live with Elizabeth when her husband of three years brought home the floosie. Floosie was what Phillida called the pseudo-blonde, willowy creature with the cornflower blue eyes.

Phillida, who had really only married so as to have a home to clean and polish and almost unlimited cooking to enjoy doing, was secretly pleased to have someone to keep Joseph 'out of her hair' as she described his amorous whims and desires.

However sharing a home, and particularly a kitchen, with someone else posed a different set of problems.

She soon discovered that the floosie also liked cooking and spent time in Phillida's personal domain, concocting what to Phillida was strong malodorous fodder in order to keep her man up to scratch.

So Phillida transferred all her personal belongings, which included her precious cooking pots and pans, to the home of her old school friend Elizabeth.

Elizabeth's home was idyllic, a white, partly thatched cottage with a large and almost unused kitchen, as well as the usual offices to clean, and the move suited Elizabeth too. She had never even entertained the notion of sullying her life with someone as large and uncouth as a man. For a start their feet were too big, and they needed almost unlimited amounts of food - which meant cooking, which was something she did only now and again from sheer necessity.

Her love was reserved for her garden, and for the great outside world, the fields and the hedges which surrounded her cottage. It also included the various animals and birds which, like her, also enjoyed the countryside.

So that when Phillida, with all her paraphernalia, descended on the cottage it seemed to be the answer to both their lives.

Being of such different dispositions and interests, they were able to avoid one another, except of course at mealtimes, and while Elizabeth enjoyed the food which had not been any trouble to her, Phillida had pleasure, when not cooking, cleaning and polishing, in looking at the garden.

There are snags and disadvantages to most situations, and when Phillida found that her friend's love of poetry was something she was expected to enthuse about, she, not unnaturally, considered the balance of their relationship needed some adjusting.

Elizabeth, unaware of any discordancy, happily quoted stanzas from her favourite versifiers wherever and whenever the occasion, as she saw it, occurred. There were, of course, poems for different seasons of the year. Wordsworth and daffodils was an obvious one, and cherry blossom simply asked for Houseman.

These Phillida accepted with a fair degree of grace, it was when Elizabeth quoted from unknown poets, such as herself, that discord began.

They were tucking into gently roasted cutlets accompanied by morning gathered carrots and onions, with mint sauce and tasty brown gravy, providing a small pool for them all to fit comfortably into, when Elizabeth quoted some stanzas which had manifested themselves to her that morning, as she had pulled a particularly healthy groundsel from between rows of tender young broad beans. Being unaware of the horrified expression on her friend's face, she was shocked when Phillida suddenly exploded "But that doesn't even rhyme!"

"It isn't meant to," Elizabeth explained gently. "It's just verse - my thoughts in verse."

Phillida, who only ever thought or spoke in good, sensible prose, grunted as she took their now empty plates out to the kitchen. She was still scowling an hour later when, wearing her sensible shoes, she strode to the village shop to buy some more washing-up liquid. The prospect of spending time each day with someone - even a good friend - who persisted in uttering words which made no sense at all . . . . . . , but on the other hand, neither was moving away appealing. And if so, where?

In a different direction, Elizabeth sought consolation in her favourite meadows and sat beneath the oak tree which she always considered to be her own, and explained the situation to its understanding branches and leaves.

She didn't expect an answer from the tree and was surprised when a voice said, not loudly but quite succinctly, "I can see that you do have a problem."

It was not a loud voice, as she might have expected an oak tree to have, and was neither male nor female. Just, she thought, gentle and understanding, as well as comforting, so she filled in a few details - how she and Phillida shared their home. Just in case the oak tree might offer a solution and ease their now rather strained relationship.

It was a good ten minutes later when the voice from the tree spoke again. "Do you mind if I come down?" it asked. "This branch is comfortable for a while, but I believe we can continue our conversation more easily if we are on the same level."

He was a slight man, neither too tall nor too short, and she saw with relief, he was not scruffy, just casually put together. He had a few scratches from too close contact with the tree, but she knew they would heal quickly after a wash and application of soothing ointment.

Phillida was home and the washing-up liquid tidily stored away; she immediately dealt with the scratches and they all settled to enjoy tea and Phillida's victoria sponge cake.

Being three of them made conversation more interesting and the stressful lunch time, a thing of the past.

Noel told them he had arrived in the village that morning, and, it being a lovely sunny day, wandered around the fields before searching for somewhere to stay. Being of a reclusive nature, the oak tree appealed to him as a sheltered place, and at the same time friendly. So he had rested there for a while before Elizabeth arrived.

Noel confided to the two ladies that he "put together" puzzles for newspapers, "Crosswords and such," he said casually.

It seemed to Phillida and Elizabeth to be an eminently suitable way of earning a living, with the added attraction that it could be done anywhere.

And as his feet were not too big and there did not seem to be much danger of a floosie joining their homestead, he stayed with them, and enjoyed Phillida's cooking and sometimes weeded a patch of garden, and even occasionally sat in the oak tree to ponder about one of his puzzles.

And they all probably lived happily ever after.

Ebb And Flow

It had been high tide but now the river turned, obeying the call back to the sea, as it had done countless centuries before. Today there was no hurry. Autumn sun glinted on the ripples as it drifted lazily by.

She sat on a bench and watched, in her mind looking back, remembering the river in all its moods. Sometimes, as today, at peace with itself, drifting slowly in the sunshine. But at others, agitated, unsure, perhaps struggling against stronger forces. And there were days when the river was excited, sweeping small craft and lesser objects before it, lapping over its banks and rushing through unprotected doorways. To her it was always interesting.

She shifted her position on the slatted bench, the sun warm on her back. Behind her on the other side of the quay, people, mostly visitors, she thought, were peering into shop windows or emerging from doorways, their arms and bags full of fripperies, gifts to take home for families and friends.

She remembered when the shops had been full of necessities, fish, fresh fruit, groceries, but two large supermarkets had changed all that. It was progress, she supposed, and wondered if her parents and grandparents had felt the same way about changes in their days.

Her eyes focused on the two ships which had docked at high tide. Now they were busy unloading, their cargoes neatly stacked on the quayside, awaiting collection.

She glanced up as a tall, well-built man approached, he was leaning heavily on a sturdy cane.

"Mind if I sit?" His voice was deep and not of the local burr.

She moved along the bench making room for him. "Please do." She smiled her welcome.

For a while they sat in companionable silence. "I used to row here," he remarked casually.

"I thought you looked an athlete," she said.

"Used to be," he grimaced. "We won many trophies on this river."

"And on others too?" she prompted him.

"We were a good team, but this is the river I remember best. You live here?" he asked, not really interested to know.

"Years ago, not now. Just visiting," she replied.

He was silent for a while, then: "I remember the regattas," he was reminiscing, half talking to himself. "And the dances afterwards – and the fair!" He laughed. "Do you remember the fair? Roundabouts of galloping horses, sliding on the mat?"

"I remember," she said. "They were fun."

"They were good times!" He spoke slowly now as if dredging his memory. "Once there was this girl, lovely she was, and interesting too. The fellows ribbed me for dancing with her so much. I wanted to see her home, but she had gone. Looked for her next day at the fair but . . ." the traffic behind them for a moment blotted out his voice. He said "But I've sometimes wondered."

She added, "What if? I think we all wonder about that."

He turned and looked across the road. "Ah, there's my wife." His ash cane helped him to his feet. "Nice meeting you," he said.

She watched him cross to where a cheerful woman waved a bag full of bright toys, to take home to grandchildren she supposed.

For a while she sat there, not now watching the river, her mind recalling long ago events and people. How strange, she thought as, like him, she pictured the regattas and the dances.

In her mind seeing again the tall young athlete who danced so well. And, as with him, she wondered "What if?"

Printed in the United Kingdom by
Lightning Source UK Ltd., Milton Keynes
140491UK00002B/13/P

9 781438 977676